Just Another Ordinary Day

ROD CLEMENT

HarperCollinsPublishers

It was the beginning of just another day.
As the first rays of sunlight slid under the door,
Amanda awoke to the sound of her alarm,
which rang at 6:30 A.M. every school day.

She took her time getting dressed
because there were so many buckles and buttons.

Then she packed her books and pencils into her backpack before flying downstairs for breakfast.

She was never very hungry in the mornings.
All she could eat was one boiled egg
and two pieces of toast.

Every morning she got a lift to school
with Mrs. Ellsworth.
Mrs. Ellsworth was the oldest person on the block
and told amazing stories about life in the old days.
She also drove the oldest car in the world, so
they were never on time.

Amanda hated being late for school.
They made such a fuss
about opening the school gate.

She liked science with Mr. Wilson.
He would often put away the books and spend the whole morning doing experiments.

At lunchtime Amanda discovered
she hadn't packed her sandwiches.
Luckily she had just enough money
to buy some lunch from the cafeteria.

Later Amanda and her friends
talked to Sue, the new girl,
who told them stories about
her home in a land far away.

In the afternoon Amanda's class went to the school library.
She loved hearing Mrs. Billops read aloud
from her huge collection of pirate stories.
Tilly Wyman was caught chewing gum again
and was sent outside.
Mrs. Billops was very upset.

When school was over,
Amanda's mom picked her up
in their off-road vehicle for
the rough ride back home.

When they finally arrived home,
Amanda and her mom
took a shower to wash off the dust.

H er dad decided to make some curry for dinner.
As usual it was just a little too hot.

After dinner Amanda curled up with a book
and her cat, Fluffy, in front of the fire.
Fluffy purred loudly on her lap.
He loved to cuddle.

It was the end of the day,
just like any other ordinary day,
but it was exhausting just the same.
As Amanda drifted off to sleep,
her father gently picked her up
and carried her upstairs to bed.

After your ordinary day,
you'll need some sleep too.

Originally published by HarperCollins Publishers, Australia.

Just Another Ordinary Day
Copyright © 1995 by Rod Clement
Printed in the U.S.A. All rights reserved.

Library of Congress Cataloging-in-Publication Data
Clement, Rod.
  Just another ordinary day / Rod Clement.
     p.   cm.
  Summary: Amanda's ordinary day has her riding to school with a Tyrannosaurus rex, having
lunch with an alien, sailing a pirate ship at library, and riding home on an elephant.
  ISBN 0-06-027666-5. — ISBN 0-06-276673-3 (lib. bdg.) — ISBN 0-06-443500-8 (pbk.)
  [1. Animals—Fiction.   2. Schools—Fiction.   3. Humorous stories.]   I. Title.
PZ7.C59114Ju   1997   96-43611
[E]—dc20   CIP
                                                                                     AC

❖
Visit us on the World Wide Web!
http://www.harperchildrens.com